DOLPHIN ISLAND

Lost in the Storm

by Catherine Hapka
illustrated by Petur Antonsson

SCHOLASTIC INC.

ISBN 978-1-338-29019-6

10 9 8 7 6 5 4 3 2 1 19 20 21 22 23

Printed in U.S.A. 40
First printing 2019

Book design by Lizzy Yoder

DOLPHIN ISLAND

Lost in the Storm

1
Storm Warning

Abby Feingold stepped out of the woods into the sheltered cove. The water was calm, ruffled only slightly by the breeze coming off the ocean.

"Anybody here?" Abby called. She took another step toward the rocky shore's edge. "Dolphins? Yoo-hoo!"

She let out a loud whistle. A second later, a sleek gray head popped into view.

Abby smiled. "Rascal!" she called. "I'm glad the weather report didn't scare you away."

A gust of wind blew her wavy brown hair into her

face. Abby pushed it back, squinting out at the dolphin. He was bobbing in the water, watching her with his big, dark eyes. Where were the others?

She got her answer a moment later when five more dolphins popped into sight. One of them, Echo, leaped up and dove back into the water with a splash.

Abby laughed. "Do it again," she called, pulling her phone out of her pocket. "I told Daddy and Rachel I'd take some photos for the resort's website."

Abby lived on Barnaby Key, a small island in the Florida Keys. The island had been a wedding gift from a relative to her father and brand-new stepmother. Now Abby, Daddy, and Rachel lived there full-time and ran Dolphin Island Family Resort. The resort had only been open for a month, but Abby already couldn't imagine living anywhere else! She especially loved the cove, and the pod of dolphins that came there every day. She and her friend Bella had named all of the dolphins: Rascal, Echo, Domino, Graygirl, Nana, and Neptune.

Abby snapped some photos of the dolphins playing. They dove and jumped, doing flips and twists in the air or skimming along just below the surface. She laughed as Neptune did a loud belly flop. Just then another gust of wind almost blew the phone out of her hand.

"Wow," she said to Graygirl, who was floating near the shore. "I guess the hurricane must be getting closer."

She frowned, a little worried. She wasn't afraid of hurricanes—as a lifelong Florida girl, she had been through several. But she wasn't sure how a hurricane would affect the island and its wildlife, including the dolphins.

Then she shrugged off her worries. "Oh well," she murmured. "The forecasters don't even know if the storm is coming toward us or not."

Just then the phone buzzed in her hand. It was a text from Rachel:

Guests heading out soon—come back if u want to say bye!

"Oops." Abby realized she'd lost track of the time. That happened a lot when she was at the cove! "Sorry, guys," she called to the dolphins. "I have to go."

Echo let out a soft whistle, as if he understood what she had said. Abby smiled and whistled back. Then she turned and hurried into the woods, following the familiar trail among the palm, gumbo limbo, and buttonwood trees.

A few minutes later, she emerged into a large open area. At the center stood the main house. Six guest bungalows were scattered across the beautiful grounds. Daddy had worked as a landscaper back on the mainland, and he still loved getting his hands dirty planting all sorts of beautiful flowers, vines, and shrubs.

The house faced a sheltered lagoon with crystal-blue water and a white sand beach. At one end of the beach was the dock where Abby's family kept their motorboat, the *Kismet*. Daddy and Rachel used the boat to take guests back and forth between the resort and Key West, a large, busy island with an airport and lots of shops and restaurants, which was about three miles away.

At the moment, Daddy was fiddling with the ropes tying the boat to the pilings. The departing guests were waiting to board. Some stood on the dock with their suitcases, while others were taking a few final photos on the beach or beneath the majestic palms.

Rachel and some of the resort employees were there, too, chatting with the guests or helping with the luggage. Abby also spotted Carlos Alvarez, the eight-year-old nephew of Sofia, the resort's head cook. Occasionally, Carlos took the boat out with her from Key West, where they both lived, and spent the day on Barnaby Key.

"Hey, Carlos," Abby said, hurrying over. "Are you leaving already? I was hoping you could help us clean up everything before next week's guests get here."

Carlos tossed his dark hair out of his eyes. "I can't, sorry," he said, though he didn't sound very sorry. "I'm going back with your dad right now—I have soccer practice this afternoon."

"Oh, okay," Abby said. Then she laughed as a bright-eyed two-year-old toddled toward them, clutching a seashell in one hand. "Bye-bye, Tandi," Abby said, scooping up the girl to give her a hug. "We'll miss you!"

The girl's mother stepped forward, smiling. "Don't worry, Abby," she said. "I'm sure we'll be back soon. We had such a lovely time here!"

"Yes." The woman's husband joined them, dragging a large suitcase. He squinted at the horizon, where a few ragged gray clouds marred the blue sky. "But don't expect us next week—we're from Chicago, you know. We don't do hurricanes!"

Rachel heard them and chuckled. "Don't worry, you'll be back at the mainland well before the hurricane gets here, even if it does come this way," she assured the couple. "And I do hope you'll come back. We've enjoyed having you."

Abby's father let out a whistle. "Boat's ready to go!" he called. "We'd better get moving so you'll have plenty of time to make your flights."

The next few minutes passed quickly in a bustle of boarding and loading. The *Kismet* was fairly small, but there was enough room for all twelve guests and their belongings, plus Daddy and Carlos. Soon the boat was chugging off across the lagoon.

Abby waved until she was pretty sure the people on board couldn't see her anymore. Then she walked back toward the house with Rachel, Sofia, and the other employees.

"That was a nice group, wasn't it?" Rachel commented. She glanced at Abby. "The next batch of guests should be here in a few hours. I hear there's a girl around your age."

"Cool!" Abby said. "Where's she from?"

Rachel shrugged. "I'm not sure. I know we have some people from Orlando, Philadelphia, North Carolina, and even the West Coast in this group, but I don't remember all the details." She smiled. "There are fifteen people this time!"

Abby knew why her stepmother looked happy. The first couple of weeks they'd had only a small number of guests. But the more people heard about the island, with its beautiful beach, fun activities, and friendly pod of dolphins, the more people wanted to come!

"That's great, darling," Sofia spoke up, smiling at Rachel. She called everyone "darling." "But it means we have lots of work to do to get ready for them. Let's get to it!"

"All hands on deck!" Abby exclaimed. That was one of Daddy's favorite sayings. It meant it was time for everyone to help out.

She didn't mind pitching in and working hard. It was worth it to live in such a beautiful place!

2

Birds of a Feather

Abby was smoothing out the bedspread in one of the bungalows when she heard a shout from the direction of the beach: "I see the boat!"

She hurried outside. The *Kismet* was still way out in the ocean beyond the reef that protected the lagoon.

Rachel emerged from the bungalow next door. "Ready?" she asked Abby with a smile.

Abby nodded. "I'll get Bogart—he's part of the welcoming committee, too."

She hurried around to the back of the main house.

She and Daddy had been hard at work building an aviary there—an outdoor enclosure for her pet macaw, Bogart. They had built a large wooden frame, then covered it with wire mesh. Daddy had brought in a big dead branch that the bird could perch on, and Abby had helped plant some shrubs and other greenery. Bogart also had a food dish, several water dishes, and a few toys.

The large parrot was perched on a branch, grooming his colorful feathers with his beak. He stopped when he saw Abby coming.

"Here, kitty kitty," he squawked in his loud, hoarse voice.

Abby laughed. She was still discovering new words and phrases that Bogart knew how to say. It had only been a few weeks since she'd rescued him after his previous owner had released him into the wild. Luckily, Daddy and Rachel had said she could keep him, and now he was the resort's official mascot.

"Come on, Bogart." Abby stretched her arm up so the macaw could hop onto it. "We have guests to greet!"

She headed around the house to the beach. By then, Daddy was steering the boat up to the dock.

"Welcome to Dolphin Island Family Resort!" Rachel called, waving to the people crowded into the boat.

Abby smiled and scanned the visitors. There was a group of four giggling women in their early twenties, several couples of various ages, and young parents with a sleepy-looking baby. There was also a tall, tanned man wearing a fishing hat, who was sitting beside a girl with short blond hair.

As the guests climbed out of the boat, Abby stepped toward the girl. "Hi, I'm Abby," she said. "I heard we had a guest around my age coming this week—I'm eight."

"I'm nine." The girl smiled. "My name's Delaney Durand, and this is my dad."

She pointed to the tanned man, who smiled and said hello before turning away to grab their luggage.

"Is that a real parrot?" Delaney asked, staring at Bogart.

"This is Bogart." Abby stroked the bird's feathers. "He's a blue-and-gold macaw."

"Cool!" Delaney looked impressed. "I don't have any pets. My mom is allergic to everything."

"Is your mom here?" Abby glanced around.

Delaney quickly shook her head. "My mom and dad are divorced," she said. "I live with my mom most of the time. But every summer before school starts, Dad and I go someplace fun where he can fish and I can do other interesting stuff."

"Well, you came to the right place." Abby smiled. "There are tons of fish around here—and lots of fun!"

"Fun, fun," Bogart croaked out. "I'm a pretty bird!"

Delaney laughed. "Did you teach him to say that?"

Abby shook her head. "I've only had him a short

time." She started to explain, but Daddy had called for attention.

"We'll be showing you all to your bungalows shortly," he said. "There will be a welcome reception in the dining pavilion after that. But first, I've already had a few questions about the possible hurricane."

"Oh dear, I was going to ask about that," said the woman with the baby. "Are we in danger?"

Rachel stepped forward to stand beside Daddy. "Not at the moment, no," she said. "The storm is still pretty far away. We'll be keeping a close eye on the forecast over the next couple of days."

"That's right." Daddy nodded. "It's too early to say whether it might come here or miss us completely. But of course we'll refund anyone who wants to leave—just in case."

3

Staying or Going?

Abby held her breath after Daddy's announcement. Would any of the guests want to leave the resort right now? She hoped not!

The woman with the baby traded a worried look with her husband. The group of young women giggled and poked one another.

"We're staying!" one of them exclaimed.

"Whoo!" her three friends cheered.

"I've never been in a hurricane," Delaney said, sounding a little worried.

Her father heard her and looked over. "Don't worry, sweetheart," he said. "Like they said, it might not even come this way."

A very tall, muscular man with a mustache nodded. "He's right," he said. "There's only about a thirty percent chance the track will cross this part of the Keys."

"Really?" Delaney looked impressed. "How do you know that?"

The tall man smiled. "I saw it on the Weather Channel," he said. "I'm a firefighter—I like to keep an eye on the conditions in the places I'm visiting. My name's Jack Milano, by the way."

The other guests started introducing themselves to one another. After that, Abby helped show everyone to their bungalows. Abby's father had named all of the bungalows after local trees and flowers. For instance, Delaney and her father were in the Silver Palm, which had two bedrooms. The four young women were in the largest bungalow, the Tamarind, while Jack the firefighter and his wife were in the Acacia Bungalow. Some of the other couples were staying in the guest rooms on the second floor of the main house.

After everyone was settled in, the guests gathered in the breezy outdoor dining pavilion between the house and the beach. Abby offered to lead a walk out to Dolphin Cove. "It's named after a pod of dolphins that likes to come there," she explained. "I can't guarantee that they'll be there right now, but they do hang out in the cove a lot."

"Cool," Delaney said. "I love dolphins!"

Several of the others guests nodded eagerly. "It would be fun to see some dolphins!" a woman with a pretty head scarf exclaimed. "Do they do tricks?"

"No, they're wild dolphins," Abby said. "But they're friendly."

Most of the guests came along to visit the cove. The parents with the baby, together with a few others, decided to stay behind.

Soon the group was stepping into the cove. The wind had died down, and the water was still. For a second, Abby was afraid that the dolphins weren't going to show up. But when she whistled, several gray heads popped into view at the far end of the cove where the cove opened into the sea.

"Wow!" Delaney exclaimed as the dolphins swam closer. "They're so beautiful!"

"That's Rascal." Abby drew attention to the large dolphin leading the way. "And the one with the spots is Domino." She pointed out the rest of the pod, too: friendly Echo, slender Graygirl, bossy Nana, and stout Neptune.

"You're so lucky to live here." Delaney crouched on the rocky shore, watching the dolphins play. "I'd love to be able to see dolphins every day. I live in California, so I see them sometimes when we go to the beach, but they're usually really far away."

"I know I'm lucky," Abby said. "Dolphins are my favorite! I love all animals, though."

"Me too." Delaney straightened up and smiled, pushing her short blond hair off her face. "I want to be a vet or a zookeeper when I grow up."

Just then Bogart dug his claws into Abby's shoulder. "Hot diggity dog!" he croaked out. Then he fluttered down to the ground and waddled toward the jungle.

"Bogart, come back!" Abby laughed and chased after the macaw. Luckily, he couldn't walk very fast. She picked him up and set him on her arm again.

"I'm a pretty bird," Bogart said.

"You're a naughty bird," Abby corrected with a smile. "Stop trying to escape."

Delaney laughed. "He's cool," she said. "They have a bunch of big parrots and stuff at this wildlife park I was reading about. It's in Arizona, and it sounds amazing. I'd love to go there sometime."

"Arizona—that's not very far from California, is it?" Abby said, scratching Bogart on the head. "Maybe you

should ask your dad to take you there for your next big trip."

Delaney shrugged. "I don't think he'd be interested in going there. There's no fishing nearby."

Before Abby could respond, there was a loud "ooh!" from the other guests. She looked out and saw Rascal and Echo doing side-by-side flips.

"I'm so glad we came here!" one of the guests exclaimed, grabbing her boyfriend's arm.

Delaney smiled at Abby, then reached out to give Bogart a pat. "Me too."

4

Swimming Session

When Abby got up the next morning, she felt excited. At first she was too sleepy to remember why.

Then she remembered: Bella was coming to the island today!

Abby hopped out of bed and got dressed extra fast. She was only halfway down the stairs when she heard the sounds of music, laughter, and talking coming from the kitchen. Sofia and the other workers arrived very early every morning to make breakfast. A couple of times a week, Bella rode out with them and stayed for the day. Abby had only met Bella a few weeks earlier, but the two of them were already great friends.

Abby burst into the kitchen, which as usual was warm and noisy and smelled like frying eggs and coffee and the spices that Sofia used to flavor her Cuban pastries. Perched on a stool near the stove was a petite, dark-haired girl with freckles dotting her cheeks.

"Hi!" Abby approached her. "What's new in Key West?"

Bella giggled. "I live on Stock Island, remember? I know it's right next to Key West, but it's a whole separate place."

"Whatever." Abby grinned. "Anyway, guess what. There's a guest our age this week! Her name's Delaney, and she's really nice."

She told Bella more about Delaney as they headed outside. It was still early, and only a few guests were in the dining pavilion. Abby spotted Delaney's dad, who was chatting with Firefighter Jack and his wife.

"Hi!" Abby approached him. "Where's Delaney?"

Mr. Durand looked up from his eggs. "She should be here soon," he said with a smile. "I woke her up on my way out."

While they waited, Abby and Bella helped themselves to juice and cereal. They were still eating when Delaney came up the steps into the dining pavilion. Abby waved her over and introduced her to Bella.

"Delaney's from California," she said.

"Wow." Bella smiled shyly. "I've never been to California, but it sounds cool."

Delaney smiled back. "It's not that exciting," she said. "This island is much better. I mean—dolphins!"

"I know, right?" Bella laughed. "Did Abby tell you how we found the cove?"

While Delaney ate, Abby and Bella told her the whole story. Bella and her family had come to stay during the first week the resort was open. She'd been out in the jungle bird-watching when she'd stumbled across the cove, which was hidden in an untamed part of the forest. At first she hadn't wanted Abby to tell anyone about the cove, because she was afraid the dolphins might leave if too many people came. Luckily, that hadn't happened.

"Wow," Delaney said when they finished. "I'm glad you didn't keep the cove a secret. Because I want to spend the whole week there watching the dolphins!"

"I know what you mean—I go there as often as I can." Abby blinked. "Wait—but don't you want to spend part of the week fishing with your dad?"

Delaney shrugged and picked up a piece of toast. "I don't usually go along when he's fishing," she said. "It's not that exciting."

"Oh, okay." Abby was surprised. She thought the whole reason for this trip was for Delaney and her dad to spend time together. But before she could ask about that, her own father hurried over.

"Do you girls have big plans this morning?" he asked with a smile. "Because I'll be spending a couple of hours sanding and staining the benches I built at the cove. If you want to tag along, you could go for a swim."

Bella nodded quickly. "Yes, please!" she exclaimed.

"Thanks, Daddy!" Abby added. She noticed that Delaney looked a little confused. "We're not allowed in the water unless an adult is within eyesight," she explained. "That's the number one rule around here. But if Daddy's at the cove with us, we can swim with the dolphins!"

Delaney gasped. "Are you serious? That sounds amazing! Let's go!"

Daddy laughed. "You have time to finish breakfast first," he said with a twinkle in his eye. "You might want to change into your swimsuits, too. How about if we meet at the trail in half an hour?"

Exactly half an hour later, they were heading into the woods. Bella always wore a swimsuit under her clothes when she came to the island, and Abby and Delaney had changed into theirs as well. Daddy was wearing work clothes and carrying a bucket of paint and tools. He led the way along the shady trail. It had started out as a narrow track made by animals. It was wider now, but not much. Daddy and Rachel wanted to keep things as natural as possible on this part of the island.

When they reached the cove, Daddy headed over to the benches he'd built, where guests could sit and watch the dolphins. The three girls hurried to the edge of the water.

"Are they here?" Bella wondered, squinting out over the sun-flecked water. "Here, dolphin dolphin dolphins!"

Delaney giggled. "Do they really come when you call?"

"No," Abby said. "But if they're close enough to hear us, they usually get curious and come to see what we're doing." She kicked off her sandals. "Come on, let's go in while we wait—it's getting hot already."

Delaney gasped. "There they are!"

Sure enough, the dolphins had just appeared at the

far end of the cove. As the three girls waded in, the dolphins swam closer. Domino did a jump, while Nana lifted her head and squeaked.

"Oh my gosh, they're so beautiful!" Delaney cried. "Will they really let us swim with them?"

"Sure," Bella said. "Just stay calm and quiet, and don't try to touch them unless they come really close."

Abby saw that her father had stopped his work to watch the pod's arrival. She waved to him. "I left my phone on my shoes," she called. "Will you take some pictures of us with the dolphins?"

"Sure thing." Daddy hurried over to grab the phone.

For the next half hour, Abby and her friends had a great time swimming with the pod. Most of the dolphins stayed just out of reach, as usual. But Echo let Delaney touch him a few times, and once, Rascal swam past so close that he bumped into Abby, making her laugh.

Finally, though, the dolphins turned and swam toward the gap leading out to the ocean. Abby treaded water and watched them go.

"Guess they're getting hungry," she said.

Bella nodded, rolling over to float on her back. "Or maybe they're heading to deeper water since they know a hurricane might be coming."

"Is that what they do?" Delaney asked. "I never really thought about what sea creatures do in a big storm."

Abby had thought about it. In fact, she'd meant to look it up, but she'd forgotten. Luckily, Bella knew all kinds of facts about the creatures who lived in the Keys.

"Yes, they'll shelter in deeper water or swim out of range if the storm comes here," Bella said.

Abby swam closer to shore until she could touch the bottom. Then she stood up and squeezed salty water out of her hair. "That's good," she said. "But I hope the hurricane doesn't come this way at all."

"Me too." Delaney shivered, even though the air

and the water were warm. "Hurricanes sound really scary!"

"Not as scary as those California wildfires I saw on the news," Bella said. "Those looked terrible!"

"They were—my grandparents had to evacuate their house for a week or so." Delaney shrugged. "Their neighborhood was okay in the end, though. Have you guys been in a hurricane before?"

"Sure, hurricanes hit Florida pretty often. Most of them aren't that bad, though. Especially if you have hurricane shutters and stuff." Abby waded out to dry ground. "Anyway, we shouldn't worry about it until we find out if it's coming this way."

5

Abuelo's Tale

The next morning, Abby walked into the busy kitchen. Sofia was stirring something on the big stove.

"Darling, can you take out another pitcher of orange juice, por favor?" the cook called. "I have my hands full."

"Sure." Abby grabbed the ice-cold pitcher and carried it outside. Rachel was in the pavilion stacking coffee cups.

"Morning, Abs," Rachel said. "Have you seen your father? I want to tell him about the latest weather report."

"What did it say?" Abby asked. "Is the hurricane coming here?"

"It turned overnight, so it looks more likely to head this way. But they're not sure yet." Rachel patted Abby on the shoulder. "There's still plenty of time if we decide to evacuate the island."

"Evacuate?" Abby felt a twinge of alarm. "Where would we go?"

Rachel shrugged. "The mainland, probably. Your aunt and uncle in Fort Myers said we could stay with them."

"But what about Bogart?" Abby exclaimed. "We can't leave him here!"

"Don't worry, we wouldn't do that," Rachel assured her. "Your father already checked, and he's welcome, too."

Abby was relieved that Bogart would be safe, no matter what. And thanks to Bella, she knew that the dolphins would be okay, too. But she still felt worried. What would happen to all the other animals on Barnaby Key?

Just then Daddy walked into the pavilion, chatting

with Firefighter Jack. Rachel hurried over to tell him about the forecast.

Meanwhile, Abby spotted Delaney and her dad eating breakfast. She walked over.

"You guys are here early," Abby said with a smile. "Sofia hasn't even sent out the tostones yet—those are really yummy fried plantains."

Mr. Durand chuckled. "I can't lie around in bed all day when the fish are jumping," he said with a wink. He glanced at his daughter. "Sure you don't want to come along, sweetheart?"

"No, thanks," Delaney said. "I'll stay on the island."

Abby knew that Delaney's father was going deep-sea fishing that day. The resort had an arrangement with Carlos's family, who ran a charter fishing business, since the *Kismet* wasn't big enough for that kind of trip.

"It's a good thing you're going fishing today instead of

waiting until later in the week," Abby told Mr. Durand. "Rachel says the storm is turning this way, maybe."

Delaney's eyes widened in alarm. "Really? What will you do if that happens?"

Before Abby could answer, there was a shout from the direction of the dock. "It sounds like the fishing boat is here," Abby said.

Mr. Durand took one last gulp of coffee, then stood up. "Great," he said. "Last chance to change your mind, Delaney."

Delaney shook her head. Moments later, her father was hurrying toward the dock along with Firefighter Jack and one of the young couples.

Abby and Delaney walked to the edge of the pavilion. They could see the dock from there. Carlos's uncle was tying up one of the family's fishing boats, a large power catamaran called the *Wahoo*. A few other people were climbing out.

"Hey, look, Carlos came again," Abby said. She squinted at the stooped figure behind Carlos. "That must be his grandfather. Carlos said he wanted to see the dolphins."

She hurried down the steps and along the white shell path to the dock. Delaney was right behind her. They arrived just as Carlos and his grandfather reached the beach.

"Hi, Abby," Carlos said. "This is my abuelo."

Carlos's grandfather looked a little like him, but much older. The edges of his eyes and mouth crinkled when he smiled. "Encantado, Abby," he said. "I've heard so much about you and this place." He glanced around. "It reminds me of when I lived in Cuba as a boy."

"It's nice to meet you, too." Abby shook Abuelo's hand and then introduced him to Delaney. "Carlos says you want to meet the dolphins. Should we go to the cove right now?"

Carlos and his grandfather agreed. Delaney decided to come, too. When they arrived, the dolphins were already there.

Abuelo let out a whistle. "¡Qué hermoso!" he murmured.

Abby understood enough Spanish to know that he was saying the dolphins were beautiful. She had to agree!

"Are you wearing a swimsuit?" she asked Carlos. "Since your abuelo is here, we can go in the water." She smiled at Abuelo. "We can only do that if an adult is watching."

"I can just wear my shorts in," Carlos said, kicking off his shoes.

He splashed into the shallow water near the shore. Some of the dolphins backed away, looking wary. But Echo swam forward with a curious squeak.

"That's Carlos," Abby called to the dolphin. "Carlos, that's Echo—he's the pod's welcome wagon."

After a moment, the other dolphins swam closer again. Soon the three kids and six dolphins were swimming around together. Abby could tell that Carlos was having a great time. He couldn't stop smiling!

Finally, Abby glanced at the shore. Abuelo was sitting on one of the benches Daddy had built, smiling and watching them play. "Let's go back and sit with him," she said to the others.

They got out and sat beside Abuelo, letting the dappled sunlight dry them off. "Thanks for sharing your dolphins with me, Abby," Abuelo said.

"You're welcome." Abby shivered as a cloud blocked the warm sun. She glanced up. "Do you think that the hurricane is coming already?"

"I hope not," Carlos said. "A hurricane can do tons of damage to a little island like this."

Abby shivered again, this time not from the cold. "What kind of damage?"

"When I was a boy, a big storm hit our small island

in Cuba." Abuelo had a faraway look in his eyes. "It took the roof off our house, and totally changed the shape of the lagoon . . ." Suddenly, he blinked and smiled. "Don't worry, Abby. There's still enough time for this storm to go a different way."

Abby hoped he was right about that. But what if the storm *did* hit the island? What if it washed away the rocks that sheltered the cove, or knocked all sorts of trees and other debris into the water? The dolphins might not be able to come here anymore!

6

What Will Happen?

That night, Abby didn't eat much of her dinner. All around her, guests were gobbling down Sofia's delicious beef stew and empanadas. Abby was too worried to be hungry.

"Something wrong with your food, Abs?" Rachel asked.

"No, it's fine." Abby took a deep breath. "I'm just worried about what will happen if the hurricane comes this way."

Rachel and Daddy traded a look. "We're worried, too," Rachel said. "But all we can do is wait and see."

"That reminds me—I should update the guests." Daddy stood up and called for attention. "We've been keeping an eye on the forecast," he said once everyone was listening. "The hurricane is getting closer, and we'll make a decision whether to stay or evacuate based on tomorrow's midday update from the weather service."

A murmur of concern rose from the guests. "Evacuate?" a woman exclaimed. "Oh dear!"

Rachel stood up beside Daddy. "We're still hoping it will turn away," she said. "But if we do have to evacuate, we'll refund your money for the rest of the week."

Most of the guests nodded. But Mr. Durand frowned. "Are you serious?" he called out. "I thought this was Florida! A little hurricane shouldn't bother anyone." He patted Delaney on the shoulder. "This is my only week with my daughter, and I intend to stay and make the most of it—hurricane or no hurricane."

Daddy looked surprised. "Oh," he said. "Well, it really would be much safer to—"

"I'm not scared," Mr. Durand interrupted loudly. "Others can run away if they want to. We're staying. Right, sweetheart?"

Delaney just shrugged and stared at her food. Abby glanced at her parents. How could they evacuate if Mr. Durand refused to leave?

Daddy cleared his throat. "Well, there's still a pretty good chance the storm will miss us. We'll have to see what happens tomorrow."

He and Rachel sat down. "What if he really won't leave?" Abby whispered, shooting a look toward Delaney and her father.

Rachel shrugged. "We'll figure it out tomorrow."

After dinner, Abby found Delaney at the buffet table looking over the desserts Sofia had just laid out. "Are you guys really going to stay even if the hurricane comes?" she asked.

"I guess." Delaney grabbed a couple of triangle-shaped guava pastries. "But never mind. It'll probably be fine—that's what your parents said, right?"

"Sure, but . . ." Abby let her voice trail off. Delaney was hurrying off toward her table.

Abby sighed and turned to help Daddy clear the dinner dishes. As he had said, they would just have to figure it out tomorrow.

The next morning, the weather was windy and overcast. Abby dressed quickly and hurried downstairs.

"It looks stormy out there," she said to Rachel, who was helping Sofia in the kitchen.

Rachel glanced out the window. "Let's just wait for that report. But it's too wet and windy to do anything outside. Maybe we should pack our bags—just in case."

Even though the dining pavilion had a roof, there were no walls, and the wind was blowing harder now.

So all the guests had breakfast in the house instead. A dozen people could fit around the big old wooden table, and the rest sat in the parlor with their plates in their laps. Everybody was talking about the hurricane. They were all eager to hear the midday update.

"Will that give us enough time to get safely back to Key West?" the baby's father asked, sounding worried.

"Yes, we'll call in a larger boat if necessary," Daddy said.

Firefighter Jack nodded. "We still have time before it gets too bad to travel," he told the others. "We don't get many hurricanes in Philadelphia, but I've volunteered during a few down south, so I know a little about how they work."

After breakfast, Abby packed some clothes, books, and other items in her suitcase. She helped Daddy fill a bag with important paperwork and computer equipment from the resort's office for safekeeping.

"What if Mr. Durand won't leave?" she asked as she zipped the bag shut.

Daddy sighed. "I guess I'll have to stay behind, too," he said. "We can't leave guests here on their own—especially ones who've never been through a hurricane before."

"I'll stay, too," Abby said quickly. "I've been through lots of hurricanes."

"I know, Absy Wabsy." Daddy smiled and ruffled her hair. "But you have to go with Rachel to the mainland. You'll want to make sure Bogart is safe, right?"

"I want to make sure you're safe, too," Abby said. She didn't like the thought of Daddy staying behind on the island. "Maybe we can convince Delaney's dad to leave, after all."

"Maybe." Daddy checked his watch. "There's still a little time before the update. Why don't you take Bogart out for some exercise? If we do evacuate, he'll be more confined than he's used to for a while."

Abby nodded and headed out to the aviary. Bogart

was huddled in a corner out of the wind. But he hopped forward when he saw her.

"Great Caesar's ghost!" he squawked. He hopped onto her arm.

Abby still felt worried as she walked out of the cage toward the edge of the woods. Were the dolphins at the cove? Or had they already headed for deeper water to hide from the storm? She wondered if she could walk to the cove and back before it was time for that weather update.

Suddenly, a gust of wind grabbed the tops of the trees, shaking them around. The wind swirled down around Abby, and her hair whipped across her face, making it hard to see.

Bogart let out a shriek of alarm. "Wait, it's okay," Abby blurted out, grabbing for him.

But it was too late. The macaw flapped into the air, tumbling around in the wind before turning and flying into the forest!

7

Where's Bogart?

"Bogart, get back here!" Abby sighed and headed into the forest. She wasn't too worried. Bogart liked to pretend to run away. But he never went far.

She expected to find him perching in a tree, or standing on the path waiting for her. But there was no sign of him. Clouds hid the sun and made everything gloomy, especially in the shady forest.

"Bogart?" Abby let out a whistle. But there was no squawk in return. "Hey, Bogart! Where are you?"

"Abby?"

Abby turned. That hadn't been Bogart calling her name—it was Delaney!

"Bogart flew away," Abby told her. "Can you help me find him? He's probably close by."

The two girls searched for the next twenty minutes. But there was still no sign of the missing macaw.

"Did you check the cove?" Delaney asked.

Abby shook her head and smiled. "Do you really think he's there? Or are you just hoping for a glimpse of the dolphins?"

Delaney giggled. "Both!"

"Okay, it's worth a look. I take him there a lot, so he might have gone that way." Abby led the way farther down the trail.

Soon they were stepping into the cove. The water looked almost as choppy as the ocean. The wind was blowing harder now, with squalls of rain every few seconds. There was no sign of the pod.

"Yikes." Delaney blocked the rain from her face with both hands. "It's getting worse out here."

"Yes." Abby felt a stab of fear. What if the hurricane was coming—and she couldn't find Bogart before it was time to evacuate? She couldn't leave him here to face the storm on his own! "Let's go back," she said. "I want to get a raincoat and a flashlight so I can keep searching."

She and Delaney raced along the path. When they reached the house, Daddy and Rachel were in the dining pavilion. Most of the guests were there, too, eating lunch.

"Oh good, you're here," Daddy said when he spotted the girls. "The midday report just came in, and it's good news—sort of."

Rachel nodded. "The main part of the hurricane is going to miss us completely," she said, sounding relieved. Then she looked around at the guests. "But as you can see already, we're still in for some unpleasant weather. We'll have lots of rain and wind from the outer bands of the storm, especially when it passes by to our south. Some of you might want to head back to Key West to ride it out. We have a generator, but it won't be safe to stay in the bungalows during the worst of the storm."

A few minutes of discussion followed. Most of the guests decided to take Rachel's advice and go to Key West. But Delaney's dad, Firefighter Jack and his wife, and one other couple, Mr. and Mrs. Parker from Orlando, decided to stay.

"It'll be an adventure," Jack said with a wink. "I'll be able to tell the guys back in Philly that I rode out an almost hurricane!"

Daddy chuckled. "I'll get the boat ready."

"And we'll start closing up the hurricane shutters," Rachel said.

"I can help with that," Jack offered. His wife, Mr. Durand, and the Parkers offered to pitch in as well. Everyone else hurried off to pack their bags.

"Will Daddy be okay in the *Kismet*?" Abby asked, peering out at the sea beyond the lagoon. The waves looked bigger than normal.

"Yes, but only if he goes this afternoon," Rachel said. "If the rest of us decide to head over to Key West later, we'll have to call the Alvarezes to pick us up in a bigger boat."

Abby gulped. "We still might evacuate?" she said. "But Bogart is missing!" She told her stepmother what had happened.

"I'm sure he'll come back soon," Rachel said. She sounded a little distracted. "Maybe Delaney can help you keep searching. But come inside if the wind gets any worse, okay? And don't go near the water. There will be rip currents."

Delaney heard her. "What's a rip current?" she asked.

"It's a strong current that's dangerous for swimmers. Storms can make them worse," Abby explained. "Now come on—let's go find Bogart!"

She and Delaney searched and searched. But by the time Daddy returned from Key West, they still hadn't found Bogart.

"Sorry, Abs." He gave her a hug, sounding tired—and feeling very wet. "You'd better come inside now. Bogart will probably be waiting in the aviary for his breakfast in the morning."

8

Fishy Behavior

The next morning, Abby jumped out of bed early, slipped on a pair of flip-flops, and ran outside in her nightgown to check the aviary. But Bogart wasn't there.

"Oh no," she whispered, her heart sinking. It was windier than ever, though the rain had stopped for the moment. Where could the macaw be hiding?

She heard a shout. Looking toward the dock, she saw Sofia, Bella, and Carlos hurrying across the beach. The *Wahoo* was at the dock. Carlos's father was tying it up.

Abby hurried to meet Bella and the others. "Nice

outfit," Carlos said with a grin, pointing at her panda-print nightgown.

Abby ignored him. "Bogart is still missing," she told Bella and Sofia.

"Oh!" Bella's eyes widened. "My parents almost didn't let me come today because of the storm. But Sofia helped me talk them into it. Good thing, too—we have to find Bogart!"

Abby glanced at the large boat tied beside the *Kismet*. "You brought the *Wahoo* today," she said, realizing for the first time that the employees usually came in Sofia's smaller pontoon boat, not in the large fishing boat.

"Yes, it's safer," Sofia said. "The water's getting rough already. Make sure you stay off the beach, okay, darlings? And don't get too close to the water even in the cove—just in case."

"We won't," Abby said. She looked at Carlos. "Want to help us look for Bogart?"

"Sure," he said. "Let's go."

"Thanks." Abby smiled at him. "We should get Delaney, too. She helped yesterday."

They headed for the Silver Palm Bungalow. Before they got there, the door swung open. Mr. Durand emerged holding a fishing pole and dressed in shorts, sandals, and a neon-orange hat.

"Sorry," Carlos told him. "The *Wahoo* isn't here to go fishing today."

"I know." Mr. Durand shot him a sour look. "I tried to convince your father to take me out—this kind of weather should get the fish riled up. Makes for interesting fishing. But he said no." He looked at Abby. "Your dad did, too."

"It's not safe on the water today," Bella told him.

Mr. Durand rolled his eyes. "Not for amateurs, maybe. But I'm no fair-weather fisherman. If nobody will take me out there, I'll just have to take myself."

Before any of the kids could say a word, he stomped off toward the kayaks stacked near the beach.

"No way," Carlos murmured. "He's not stubborn enough to go out there in a kayak, is he?"

"Shh!" Abby elbowed him as Delaney stepped out of the bungalow. "Hey, Delaney, is your dad really going fishing today?"

Delaney shrugged. "He said he wants to catch us some lunch. I tried to talk him out of it."

Abby squinted after Mr. Durand, worried. "Maybe I should tell my parents. They can tell him not to go."

"No!" Delaney grabbed her arm. "Don't, okay? I'm sure he already told them. Anyway, he'll be really mad if he finds out we tattled."

Abby wanted to argue, but she was still worried about Bogart. Mr. Durand was a grown-up—not a helpless bird. He could take care of himself.

"Come on," she said. "Let's go find Bogart before the weather gets even worse."

9

Found and Lost

Abby and the others searched and searched. It was still windy, but luckily there hadn't been much rain all morning. That made it easier to see.

Finally, after a little over half an hour, Abby spotted a flash of bright blue and yellow in the forest just past the cove.

"Bogart!" she cried. "Guys, I think I see him!"

She rushed forward and peered up into a large tree. When she whistled, there was a loud squawk.

"Bogart!" Carlos skidded to a stop beside Abby. "What are you doing up there?"

Bella and Delaney arrived, too. "He must have gotten confused in the stormy weather," Bella said breathlessly. "I guess he couldn't find his way home and decided to roost up there."

Bogart was already hopping from branch to branch, heading toward them. "Shiver me timbers," he said in his rusty voice. "I'm a pretty bird!"

Abby laughed with relief. "Oh, Bogart, you silly bird! Let's get you home."

Soon the macaw was perched on her shoulder. "Let's hurry back," Delaney said as the wind shook the treetops above them and rain started to spatter through to the ground.

"We can take a shortcut through the cove," Bella said.

When they reached the cove, Abby glanced toward the water. The wind was blowing the waves around, but it still looked pretty calm. Then she saw a familiar sleek gray head pop into view.

"Rascal!" she exclaimed in surprise. "What are you doing here? And where are the others?"

"That's weird," Bella said. "I know the hurricane isn't coming right over us, but I thought the dolphins would go to deeper water while the weather's bad."

The big dolphin swam back and forth near the shore, staring at them. He let out a series of chirps and whistles.

"What's he doing?" Carlos wondered. "Is he confused because of the storm, like Bogart?"

"Maybe." Abby took a step closer, trying to see what the dolphin was doing.

"Careful." Bella stepped after her. "They said not to get too close to—oh!" She cut herself off with a gasp. "Look!"

Abby looked where her friend was pointing. Then she gasped, too.

"What is it?" Carlos hurried forward to join them.

So did Delaney. When she saw what the others were looking at, her face went pale. "Oh no!" she cried. "That looks like my dad's fishing hat!"

Abby stared at the neon-orange hat bobbing in the choppy water. Rascal turned and nosed it, then chirped at them again.

"How did his hat get in here?" Carlos wondered.

Delaney was already running for the path back to the beach area. "Dad!" she cried. "Hurry—we have to make sure he's okay!"

Abby raced after her, hardly noticing Bogart's claws digging into her shoulder. She pulled out her phone and called home as she ran. When her father answered, she blurted out what they'd seen.

"What?" Daddy's voice sounded startled. "He went out in a kayak on his own?"

"We thought you knew," Abby exclaimed. "Delaney said . . . well, never mind. We're coming back right now."

"Go straight inside and stay there," Daddy ordered her. "I'll take care of this."

He hung up before she could say anything else. Abby told the others what he'd said.

"He'll probably call the Coast Guard," Carlos guessed. "They can go out and search for your dad if he's lost at sea, Delaney."

Delaney didn't answer. She just put on a burst of speed.

It started raining harder as they emerged into the clearing near the beach. Abby squinted through the rain and wind, trying to spot a kayak out in the lagoon. But it didn't even look like the lagoon right now. The waves were almost as big as the ones out in the open sea!

Bogart huddled next to Abby's head, his feathers fluffed up against the weather. "Here, kitty kitty," he muttered.

"I don't see anything out there," Carlos said. He hurried along the beach, peering out at the stormy lagoon.

"I do." Bella's voice sounded funny—sort of like she was trying to talk and swallow at the same time.

When Abby turned to look, her friend was staring at something being pulled to shore by the surf.

She gasped as she realized what it was—a paddle from one of the kayaks!

10

Man Overboard

Just then a shout rang out from the direction of the house. Abby turned to see Daddy, Rachel, Mr. Alvarez, and Firefighter Jack running toward them. “Get in the house, kids!” Rachel called.

Carlos’s father was already hurrying along the dock toward the *Wahoo*, which was bobbing and swaying in the rough water. Daddy stopped on the beach, his phone in his hand.

“I called the Coast Guard,” he shouted to Abby and

the other kids over the wailing wind. "They're on the way. I'm going to wait for them here while Rachel and Jack go with Rafe to search. It's lucky the *Wahoo* was here—it's too rough for the *Kismet* already, but the larger boat should be fine."

Abby nodded and glanced along the dock. Rafe was Mr. Alvarez's first name. He was a really good boatman. Rachel used to be a lifeguard, so she would be helpful out there, too. So would Jack—firefighters knew a lot about emergencies. The two men were already boarding the *Wahoo.* Rachel was still on the dock untying the ropes. Jack stopped to help her from the deck of the boat. Mr. Alvarez disappeared into the cabin, and a second later came the roar of the motor starting up. Rachel jumped onto the boat, and she and Jack went into the cabin, too.

Delaney stepped forward. "I want to go with them."

Daddy shook his head. "You kids get inside and dry off. We'll take it from here."

"But that's my dad out there!" Delaney stared at the boat. "I want to help!"

"I'm sorry, but that's out of the question." Daddy's voice was firm. "We're doing our best to—" He stopped talking as his phone buzzed. "Excuse me, that's the Coast Guard calling back," he told the kids. Then he turned away to answer.

Abby felt helpless. She could tell that Delaney was really worried, but she wasn't sure how to help her. Bogart let out a soft squawk.

"I'd better get this guy inside," she said, giving the bird a pat. "Come on, we can have some of Sofia's hot cocoa while we wait."

She turned toward the house. Carlos and Bella hurried ahead of her. Daddy was wandering up the beach with his back to the kids, talking on the phone.

But where was Delaney? Abby turned around to check—just in time to see Delaney sprint down the dock and disappear onto the *Wahoo*!

"Delaney, wait!" she cried.

Bella heard her and turned around. "Where'd she go?"

Abby ran to her. "Here, take Bogart inside," she said, quickly transferring the macaw to her friend's arm. "Delaney is trying to stow away with the rescuers. I have to stop her!"

Without waiting for a response, she turned and raced onto the dock. The *Wahoo* was starting to move—it was inching along the dock toward the open water beyond. Delaney was nowhere in sight.

"Hey!" Abby shouted. But the wind swallowed up her voice so she wasn't sure anyone could hear it. After taking a deep breath, she leaped across the space between the *Wahoo* and the dock. Oof! She landed on the boat's slippery rear deck.

Delaney was there, too, crouched behind one of the fishing chairs. Abby crawled over to her.

"We have to get back to the dock!" she cried.

Delaney shook her head. "You can go back," she said,

looking stubborn. "I'm going to help find my dad!" She glanced at something over Abby's shoulder. "Anyway, it's too late."

Abby looked over her shoulder. The *Wahoo* had cleared the deck and was picking up speed. The dock was rapidly disappearing behind them. They couldn't get back now!

"Oh no," Abby moaned. "We're going to be in so much trouble . . ."

"So what?" Delaney said. "My dad's in huge trouble, remember? The more people looking for him, the better."

Abby didn't answer. She looked out over the side of the boat, slitting her eyes to keep out the driving rain. The *Wahoo* was already almost halfway across the lagoon. Soon they'd be on the open sea . . .

At that moment, Rachel stepped out of the cabin holding a pair of binoculars. When she saw the two girls, she looked surprised—and then furious.

"What are you doing here?" she exclaimed. "We told you to stay on the island!"

"I'm sorry!" Abby cried. "It was an accident."

"It was—for her," Delaney said. "She tried to stop me. Don't be mad at her. You can be as mad at me as you want—but only after we find my dad."

"Get in here," Rachel said, gesturing to the cabin behind her. "Maybe we can still turn back and drop you off."

But when they were all inside the boat's cozy cockpit, the adults decided it was too late. "Mr. Durand has been out there too long already," Mr. Alvarez said, pulling two life vests out of a cabinet and handing them to Abby and Delaney. "If we delay the search any longer . . ."

"Okay, you're right," Rachel agreed. "The girls will be safe as long as they stay in here." She glared at Abby and Delaney. "And stay out of the way!"

"But I want to help." Delaney sounded stubborn again. "At least give me some binoculars or something."

Mr. Alvarez dug several pairs of binoculars out of a cabinet. "The more eyes looking, the better," he said. "Jack, you take the front deck; Rachel can take the stern. I'll call back to the island and let them know these two are with us."

"Okay." Rachel glared once more at Abby and Delaney. "If you girls want to be helpful, keep watch out the side windows."

"We're on it," Abby promised. She clicked the last buckle on her life vest, then grabbed a set of binoculars.

It was hard to see much through the rain-streaked windows, but she did her best, peering out at the frothy waves. Mr. Alvarez was at the wheel, leaning forward as he steered the boat slowly past the reef and into the open sea.

When Abby looked over at Delaney, she had her binoculars pressed to her face—and tears leaking out from beneath them.

"Hey, it's going to be okay," Abby called to her. "Remember, it's not just us out here trying to save your dad."

Delaney lowered the binoculars and blinked. "What do you mean? The Coast Guard?"

"Well, yes, them too, as soon as they get here." Abby shrugged. "But I was talking about the dolphins. Rascal was the one who showed us your dad's hat, remember? And he was alone, which means the rest of the pod is probably with your dad."

Mr. Alvarez looked back at them. "You think the dolphins are out here? I've heard tales all my life about dolphins helping swimmers and boaters."

"See?" Abby smiled at Delaney. "So all we have to do is find the pod and take over the rescue from them."

Suddenly, there was a shout from the back of the boat. Rachel burst into the cabin. "Off to starboard," she told Carlos's dad. "It's hard to see, but there's definitely something in the water that way."

Abby rushed to the starboard side window and peered out. Rachel was right—even through the rain, she could see a disturbance in the water. A moment later, a familiar gray form burst into view for a second.

She gasped. "Dolphins!" she cried. "It's the pod—I knew it!"

She crossed her fingers. They'd found the dolphins. Now there was just one question. Was Delaney's dad with them?

11

Getting Closer

When the *Wahoo* got closer to the pod, Firefighter Jack let out a cry. "It's the kayak!" he said, pointing.

Abby gulped as she saw a small, bright yellow boat bobbing upside down in the waves. Delaney went pale.

"Dad?" she whispered.

Abby scanned the nearby waters. Suddenly, a dolphin bobbed into view. It was hard to see, but she thought it might be Neptune. The stout dolphin was pushing at something with his nose. Then a couple more dolphins appeared, shoving at something that looked a little like another dolphin . . .

"That's him!" Delaney shrieked. "I see him! The dolphins have Dad!"

"She's right!" Firefighter Jack leaped for the cockpit door, grabbing a coiled rope off the wall on his way.

"Stay in here, kids," Rachel ordered as she followed.

Abby was afraid that Delaney would ignore her and rush outside. So she blocked the way, grabbing the sides of the door frame. They were closer to the dolphins now, but not close enough . . .

"Let me past," Delaney cried, shoving at her.

"No—wait. I need to get the dolphins' attention." Abby took a deep breath and let out a loud, long whistle, just like the one she often used to call the pod in the cove. Out in the choppy water, she saw one of the dolphins lift its head in response. A moment later, the whole pod starting shoving Mr. Durand toward the *Wahoo*!

"We're almost there!" Rachel shouted to Mr. Alvarez, who was still at the wheel. "Cut the engine!"

Abby held her breath, watching as Rachel and Jack tossed a floating ring attached to a rope out toward Mr. Durand. It fell short, but Domino stuck his snout through the center and dragged it closer until Mr. Durand could grab it.

"They've got him!" she cried, finally stepping aside so Delaney could see.

This time Delaney didn't try to run out. She just stood there watching, tears streaming down her face and mixing with the rain blowing in through the door. Mr. Alvarez pushed past her, joining Rachel and Jack at the rail. Together, the three adults hauled Mr. Durand toward them. The dolphins stayed beside him until they'd pulled him all the way there and up onto the deck.

"Dad!" Delaney finally burst into motion. She leaped at her father, grabbing him in a huge hug.

"Sweetheart!" Mr. Durand sounded weary, but he wrapped his arms around her. "I'm so happy to see you . . ."

Abby stepped to the side of the boat and looked down. The dolphins were still there. She was pretty sure that Graygirl looked up at her and smiled. Then, with one last chirp, the whole pod dove away out of sight.

"Thanks, guys," she whispered, even though she knew they couldn't hear her. "Thanks a million."

After the *Wahoo* returned to the island, Abby ran upstairs just long enough to change into dry clothes. The others from the boat did the same. Meanwhile, Daddy, Bella, Carlos, Jack's wife, and the Parkers helped Sofia make coffee and hot cocoa and put out all kinds of food in the big front parlor. Bogart was there, too, perched in his indoor cage in the corner, his brightly colored feathers almost dry by now.

When the whole group was back together, it was

time to hear the rest of the story. Mr. Durand sat on the couch with his arm wrapped tightly around his daughter's shoulders. "I guess I messed up," he said sheepishly, glancing around at everyone else. "I knew it by the time I was halfway across the lagoon in that little kayak. But a current grabbed me, and then I lost hold of the paddle . . ."

"We saw the paddle," Carlos told him. "That's what made us so worried."

Bella nodded. "That and the hat—one of the dolphins brought it into the cove."

"Really?" Jack's wife looked surprised. "Why would it do something like that?"

"Dolphins are really smart," Abby told her. "We think he was looking for us—to let us know that Mr. Durand was in trouble."

Jack's wife and the other guests looked even more surprised. But Mr. Durand nodded.

"I think you're right," he told Abby. "The dolphins found me right after I drifted out past the reef into deeper water. That one with the spots on its back . . ."

"Domino," Bella spoke up. "We call him Domino."

Mr. Durand nodded. "Domino was the first one to appear. Then a couple of others," he said. "They gathered around the kayak—I think maybe they were trying to push me back toward shore." He shook his head. "But then a really big wave came and swamped the kayak completely. I tried to stay upright, but . . ."

He made a motion with his free hand, like a boat flipping over. Delaney shuddered.

"You must have been so scared!" she whispered.

Her father smiled. "A fisherman never gets scared," he said. Then he shrugged and sighed. "Okay, but maybe I was a little worried. Those dolphins, though—they stayed close. One of the bigger ones even let me grab the fin on top of his back to catch my breath."

Abby widened her eyes at Bella. In all the time they'd spent swimming with the pod, none of the dolphins had ever let them do anything like that!

"It was probably Echo, or maybe Rascal," Bella guessed. "They're the bravest."

"Yeah." Abby looked at Mr. Durand. "Anyway, I'm glad they found you."

"Me too." Mr. Durand glanced around. "And I'm sorry I acted like a jerk, going out alone like that without telling anyone. I put myself in danger, and worse, I put all of you in danger, too. Without those dolphins . . ."

"Never mind," Daddy spoke up. "We're just glad you're safe."

"Me too," Delaney said in a small voice.

Her father looked down at her. "I put you in danger, too," he said, sounding choked up all of a sudden. "What if the hurricane had hit the island after all, and I made you stay here? I'm sorry, Delaney. I guess

I'm just a stubborn guy. But I learned my lesson this time."

"It's okay." Delaney shrugged. "And if you'd rather just go on a fishing trip by yourself next summer . . ."

"What?" Her father leaned back, staring at her. "By myself? I thought you liked our summer trips!"

"I do," Delaney said. "But I know you want to go fishing on your vacations. That's why we always go to places like this, right?"

Her father looked confused. "I thought you liked places like this. That's why I picked it—nothing to do with fishing."

"I do like it here." Delaney glanced around with a small smile. "At least when there's not a hurricane passing by . . ."

Abby laughed, but she was starting to figure something out. "Hang on," she spoke up. "Don't you guys decide where to go together? I thought that's what Delaney said when you first got here."

"Sort of," Delaney said.

"No," her father replied at the same time, frowning slightly. "Delaney always says she's happy going wherever I want to go. So I end up guessing what she'll like . . ." He sighed. "It's not easy to figure out, you know, sweetheart. I don't see you enough to know you as well as I'd like. Did you really think I just wanted to go fishing?"

"Maybe. Sort of. I don't know." Delaney bit her lip. "I just wanted to do stuff you liked so you'd want to keep doing our trips."

"Of course I want to keep doing them!" Mr. Durand said. "In fact, I was talking to your mother about seeing you more often."

"Heavens to Betsy, that's good potato salad!" Bogart squawked suddenly, which made everyone laugh—and relax a little.

"You're a silly bird, Bogart," Abby said.

"I'm a pretty bird," Bogart replied with a shake of his feathers.

"Well, the past is the past, as my granny always said," Rachel added. "Maybe in the future, you two can choose your vacations together."

"No way," Mr. Durand said. "I've had to choose the past few years. Next summer, Delaney has to pick where we go. Even if there's not a fish within a thousand miles!"

"Really?" Delaney shot a sidelong look at her father. "Because there's this wildlife park in Arizona I kind of wanted to check out . . ."

"We're there," her father said with a smile. "But why wait for summer? Arizona is close to home—we'll go there on your first school vacation!"

A sudden crack of thunder drowned out whatever Delaney said next—and made everyone jump. Abby looked out the nearest window, which was covered by a hurricane shutter made of clear, thick material. She could see through it, but everything looked a little cloudy and wavy.

"It's getting worse out there," Rachel said. "Time to finish battening down the hatches."

Daddy was already heading for the door. "Who wants to help get the boats on shore? Rafe, I don't think you'd better try to get back to Key West right now."

Mr. Alvarez nodded. "Carlos, Bella, Sofia, looks like we're riding it out here," he announced. "Carlos, text your mother so she can let everyone know we're staying. Then let's get those boats safe."

Everyone scattered in different directions to prepare before the storm got even worse. Abby helped Rachel bring clean towels and sheets upstairs from the laundry room, since all the guests would be staying in the main house instead of the bungalows during the storm.

"Your father says you kids knew Mr. Durand was heading out there alone," Rachel said in a serious voice as she dropped a stack of towels in one of the second-floor bathrooms. "Why didn't you say something sooner?"

Abby bit her lip. "I wanted to, but Delaney said we shouldn't. She said her dad would think we were tattletales."

Rachel turned to face her. "It's not tattling if someone's life could be in danger," she said. "You understand that, don't you?"

"I do now," Abby replied. "I promise."

"Good." Rachel smiled and gave her a quick hug. "Now let's get back downstairs and see what else needs doing."

12

Aftermath

". . . and then Rascal disappeared for a second, but then he leaped out of the water—pow!" Abby made a bursting motion with her fingers to demonstrate. "He leaped all the way up in the air—right over Neptune and Graygirl!"

Firefighter Jack chuckled. "Rascal must be the Evel Knievel of dolphins."

"Who?" Bella asked, sounding as confused as Abby felt.

"Evel Knievel was a famous daredevil who used to jump his motorcycle over all sorts of stuff," Jack explained. "Cars, trucks, buses—he even tried to jump a steam-powered rocket over a canyon once."

"Really? Cool!" Carlos looked impressed. "Can I borrow your phone, Abby? I want to see if there are any videos of that stuff online."

His father raised his eyebrows. "Don't get any ideas, son," he said as the other adults laughed.

While Carlos looked up videos, Abby and Bella told more dolphin stories. It was almost dinnertime, and the storm was still raging outside. Occasionally an especially strong wind gust made the whole house shake. But the parlor was warm, dry, and cozy with all the people gathered there. Delaney and her father were still sitting together on the sofa. Carlos was sprawled on the floor in front of the fireplace. Jack, Daddy, and the Parkers sat at one of the tables playing cards. Everyone else was sipping coffee or cocoa and listening to the girls' dolphin stories.

"Here, kitty kitty!" Bogart burst out suddenly.

Abby looked over at him as everyone laughed. "That's his favorite phrase lately," she said. "I'll have to start teaching him some new things to say."

"How about 'Welcome to Dolphin Island'?" Bella suggested.

"Good idea!" Abby smiled at her. "He already thinks he's part of the welcoming committee, after all."

Her smile faded as she glanced at the window just in time to see a large palm frond blow past outside. They might not be in the direct path of the hurricane, but the storm was pretty bad out there. What if the wind or the waves changed the cove? Would the dolphins come back if that happened?

Bella was telling a story about Echo and Domino playing tag. Abby did her best to pay attention and not worry about what was happening outside. She would just have to wait and see what happened after the storm passed.

When Abby woke up the next morning, bright sun was streaming in through the hurricane panel over her window. The storm was over!

By the time she was dressed and downstairs, most of the others were out on the porch. "How does it look?" Abby asked as she joined them.

"Hard to tell." Daddy peered from a soggy fallen palm frond on the porch steps to a stray plastic bag tangled in a shrub. "Let's walk around and have a look."

Leaves and other debris lay everywhere, covering the white shell paths and strewn across the floor of the dining pavilion. Daddy was going to have to fix some of the plantings, and the Orchid Bungalow had shingles missing and a little bit of water damage inside.

Even so, Daddy and Rachel seemed relieved. "I'm so thankful we didn't get a direct hit," Rachel commented, kicking at a wad of seaweed near the dock.

"Can we check the cove?" Abby asked, still feeling anxious. "Please?"

Daddy and Rachel traded a look. "Sofia's already starting breakfast," Daddy said. "But if you promise to hurry straight there and back . . ."

"Thanks!" Abby cried without waiting to hear the rest.

She raced inside to find Bella, Delaney, and Carlos. Soon the four of them were hurrying along the trail through the forest. It was harder to follow than usual. The ground was littered with twigs and leaves, and a small tree had fallen across it in one spot.

Finally, they emerged into the cove. The morning sunlight glinted off the still water, which had more leaves and twigs floating on it. Abby scanned the shore and the opening into the sea. All the big rocks were still in their usual places, and nothing else seemed different.

"Where are the dolphins?" Delaney wondered.

Bella looked a little worried. "Maybe we should try whistling for them," she suggested.

Abby took a deep breath and let out a whistle. For a second, nothing happened, and her heart sank. Were the dolphins gone for good?

But then a sleek gray head popped into view—and then another, and another. Soon the entire pod was there, swimming toward shore!

"Hooray!" Abby cheered. "They're here!"

"Cool," Carlos said. "Now let's go back before my dad eats all the sausages."

When Abby and her friends returned to the house, they told the adults about seeing the dolphins.

"Wonderful," Rachel said.

"Yes, what a relief." Daddy chuckled. "I'd hate to have to rename the resort again."

Abby grinned at him, knowing he was only teasing. The resort had the perfect name, and the perfect pod of dolphins to go with it.

"You'd better not rename it," Delaney said with a smile. "Because I decided where I want to go for next summer's father-daughter trip." She glanced at her dad. "Right back here—to Dolphin Island Family Resort!"

Read on to discover how the adventures at Dolphin Island began!

A Daring Rescue

"Look, Abby! Dolphins!"

"Where?" Abby Feingold raced over to her stepmother, Rachel, who was standing with her bare feet in the surf. It was a beautiful, hot, sunny summer day in the Florida Keys. Abby and Rachel were on the beach looking out across the peaceful lagoon at the sea between their island and Key West.

Yes, *their* island. Abby still could hardly believe that her family owned an island now! It had happened a few months ago when Daddy and Rachel got married.

Rachel's great-aunt Susan had given them this island, which was called Barnaby Key, as a wedding gift. Great-Aunt Susan had lived there for many years, and Rachel had loved visiting when she was Abby's age. But for the past ten years, Great-Aunt Susan had lived with her son in Miami, and nobody had lived on the island.

"Where are the dolphins?" Abby squinted to see past the sunlight glinting off the waves. Then she gasped. "Oh, I see them now!"

She held her breath and watched the dolphins. There were four or five of them—it was hard to tell, since they never stayed still. They leaped out of the water one after the other, seeming to play tag.

"They're beautiful, aren't they?" Rachel said. "I love dolphins."

"Me too." Abby smiled up at her new stepmother. Daddy always said that Rachel was the best thing to happen to him since Abby was born. Abby had to agree. She already couldn't imagine their family without her. Rachel was kind and smart and always smiling. Her father was from Jamaica, and Rachel had lived there until she was a little older than Abby was now. Rachel's voice still had a lilting accent that sounded like everything she said was a song.

Then Abby returned her gaze to the dolphins. She watched them jump and twist and play. One of the dolphins was a little smaller than the others. It leaped right over a bigger dolphin, then popped back up, seeming to laugh.

"I hope Daddy gets back in time to see the dolphins," Abby said, pushing aside a strand of wavy brown hair that the sea breeze had blown into her face.

"That would be nice," Rachel agreed. "I bet our guests would love seeing dolphins, too. Maybe we can add a dolphin-spotting boat trip to the schedule. What do you think?"

"That's a great idea." Abby took out her phone and

made a note of it. She'd received the phone for her eighth birthday, which had happened a few weeks after the wedding. Daddy said she was the most responsible just-turned-eight-year-old he knew, and that she deserved to have her own phone. Besides, living on an island, she might need it.

Next, Abby took a few photos of the dolphins. But they were pretty far away—when she looked at the photos, the dolphins looked like tiny gray dots.

"Oh well," she said. She stuck the phone back in the pocket of her shorts. "Maybe they'll come closer to the beach sometime."

"Maybe," Rachel agreed. "Anyway, I'm glad we saw them. I've always thought they were good luck. Maybe seeing them is a good sign for our brand-new resort!"

Don't miss any of the Dolphin School books!

#1: Pearl's Ocean Magic

#2: Echo's Lucky Charm

#3: Splash's Secret Friend

#4: Flip's Surprise Talent

#5: Echo's New Pet

#6: Pearl's Perfect Gift

#7: Flip's Great Escape

#8: Splash's Big Heart

M T ANG R

A time-traveling golden retriever with search-and-rescue training . . . and a nose for danger!

SCHOLASTIC

scholastic.com

RANGER1